MORE OF BRER RABBIT'S TRICKS

DRAWINGS BY EDWARD GOREY

MORE OF BRER RABBIT'S TRICKS

ENNIS REES

Hyperion Paperbacks for Children
New York

Text © 1968 by Ennis Rees.
Illustrations © 1968 by Edward Gorey.
All rights reserved.
Originally published in 1968 by Young Scott Books.
Published in 1989 by Hopscotch Books™,
A Division of WaterMark, Inc.
Printed in the United States of America.
For information address Hyperion Books for Children,
114 Fifth Avenue, New York, New York 10011.

First Hyperion Paperback edition: March 1994

1 3 5 7 9 10 8 6 4 2

Rees, Ennis.
More of Brer Rabbit's tricks/by Ennis Rees; illustrated by
Edward Gorey— 1st Hyperion Paperback ed.
p. cm.
Summary: A retelling in rhymed text and illustrations of three
tales about the antics of Brer Rabbit and his friends.
ISBN 1-56282-578-X (pbk.)
1. Afro-Americans—Folklore.   2. Tales—United States.
[1. Folklore, Afro-American.   2. Folklore—United States.
3. Animals—Folklore.]   I. Gorey, Edward, ill. II. Title.
PZ8.3.R254Mo   1994
813'.4—dc20   93-32676   CIP   AC

NOTE

For many years, people in the American South have told stories about Brer Rabbit, dozens and dozens of them. Some children in the South, long before they learn to read, still hear these stories from adults. But fewer and fewer people seem to know them nowadays, mostly because of the difficult dialect in which they were originally recorded. This is a pity, for the Brer Rabbit stories are among the best folktales we have.

Since the language of the original Southern versions has all the wit and richness of good poetry, I have here selected three of my favorite Brer Rabbit stories and attempted to re-create them in rhyming verse. Of course I hope these story poems in modern English will be enjoyed for themselves, but if they also serve to lead the reader on to older collections of dialect tales about Brer Rabbit, so much the better.

Versions of many of these stories have been told all over the world in many different languages for countless generations, but especially in Africa. And Brer Rabbit is what students of folklore call a "trickster." There are many tricksters in the stories of different peoples from Asia and Africa to America. Sometimes they take the form of a man, but often that of a spider, a raven, a coyote, or some other creature. For us Brer Rabbit is the funniest and most effective trickster of all, and he remains our best example of how the small and weak can often outwit and thereby triumph over the large and powerful and hungry. But not always. Once in awhile, Brer Rabbit is too smart for his own good, and so gets the worst of it.

In the stories, Brer Rabbit's other name is Riley, and his children are sometimes called "the little Rabs," for short.

ENNIS REES
Columbia, S.C.

BRER FOX BAGS A LESSON

Now Brer Fox at last became rather scared
Of Brer Rabbit's tricks, and he no longer dared
To come right out and chase the good Riley.
He still tried to catch him, but tried more slyly.
He'd even drop by and try to pretend
That he was Brer Rabbit's very best friend.

One day he asked Brer Rabbit to go
And hunt some with him, but Riley said no,
He felt sort of lazy and trifling that day
And wanted just to while it away.
So Brer Fox went out and hunted alone
While Riley nibbled his carrots and pone.
   But along toward sundown he found a good spot
To wait for Brer Fox and see what he got.
And pretty soon he came striding along,
Happily whistling his favorite song.

At this Riley wondered, because he could see
That Brer Fox's gamebag was flat as could be.
But what was that he had under one arm?
A big piece of cheese he had got from some farm.
Brer Fox had been robbing old Mr. Man,
And right away Riley made up a plan,
For he just happened to be in the mood
For some of that cheese to go with his food,
And he got word direct from his palate
To get some cheese to put in a salad.

So he hopped out and lay down in the road
Where Brer Fox would pass with his ill-gotten load,
And there Riley lay, from tail to head
Stretched out as stiff as if he were dead.
When Brer Fox saw him, he turned him around
And looked at him closely there on the ground.
"Now what in creation is this?" he said.

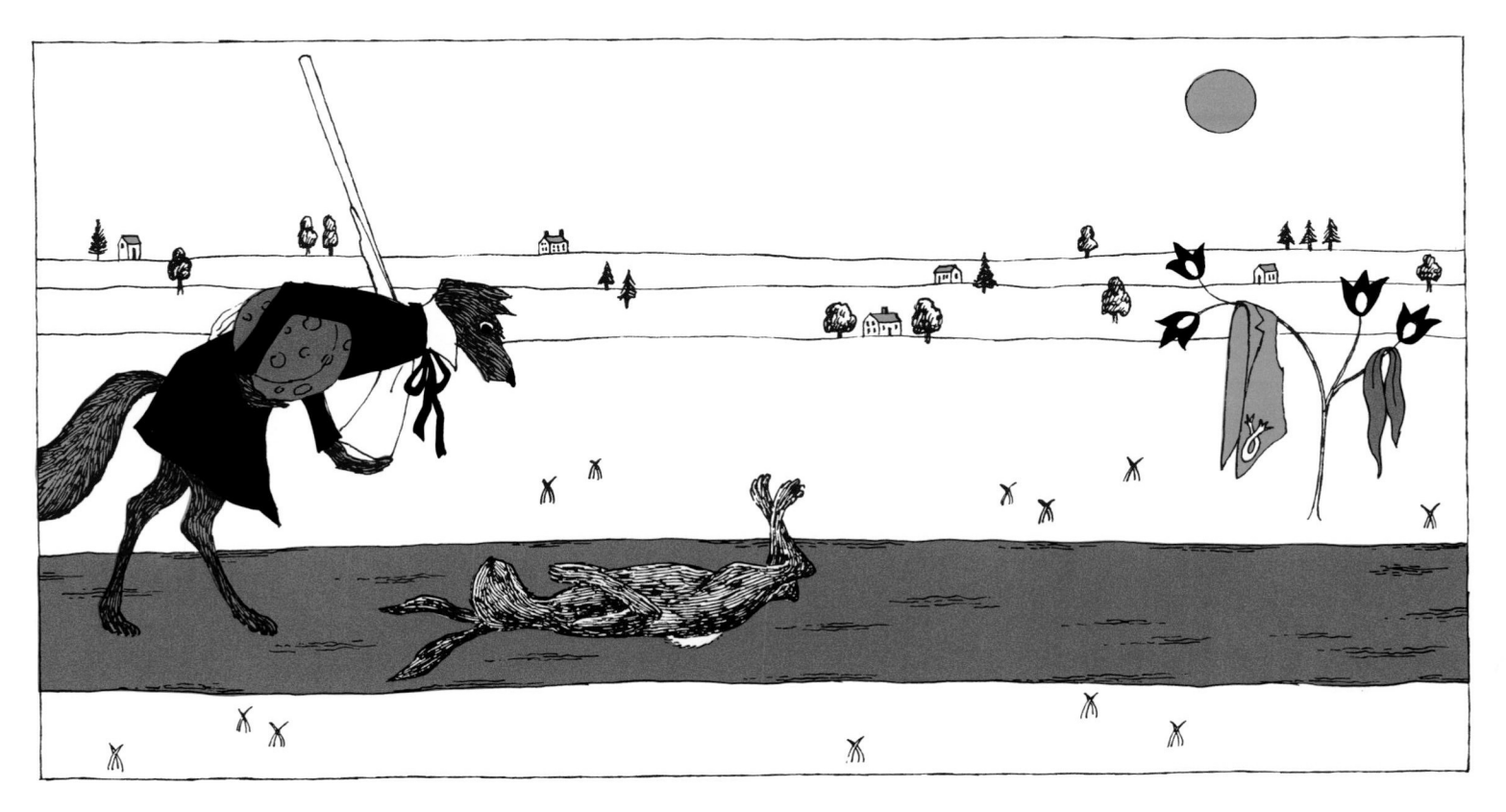

"I wonder how long this rabbit's been dead.
He's almost the fattest rabbit ever—
But I wouldn't eat him, never, never."
So saying, he struck up his whistling tune
And after a bit more thinking he soon
Set out down the road, but was no sooner gone
Than Riley was up and traveling on.

In a minute or two he got up ahead
Of whistling Brer Fox, and again he played dead,
Lying out there in the road just as if
His last hour had gone and now he was stiff.
Well when Brer Fox saw another dead rabbit,
He said to himself, "I'm just going to grab it,
And now I'll go back and get that other
That looks so much like this rabbit's brother."

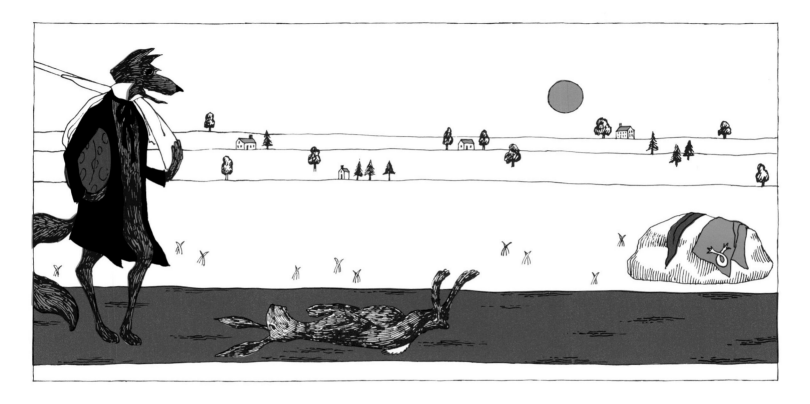

I don't suppose they've been dead long,
And not to eat them would surely be wrong,
Especially when they're the fattest ever.
I just couldn't waste them, never, never.
Then too, when folks see such rabbits as these,
Along with this piece of Mr. Man's cheese,
They'll say I'm old Hunter from Huntersville.
Yes-sir-ee, that they will!"

So Brer Fox put down his gamebag and cheese
Right beside Brer Rabbit's stiff knees
And loped on back to where he thought
Another rabbit was already caught.

But he was no sooner out of sight
Than Riley hopped up with enormous delight,
And putting that cheese in Brer Fox's bag,
He set out for home to have a good brag.

The next day Brer Fox still tried to pretend
That he was Riley's faithfulest friend,
And when Riley asked him what he had bagged,
He said, "A good lesson," as low his tail dragged,
And right then he paid for part of his sins
With a dreadful case of the awful dry grins.

FISHING FOR SUCKERS

One hot summer's day, Brer Fox, just by habit,
Was trailing along behind Brer Rabbit,
Hoping to take him somewhere by surprise,
When all at once he blinked both his eyes
At what he saw Riley suddenly do,
And what Riley did was strange, it is true.

The day was so hot he was nearly cooking,
And so Brer Rabbit had long been looking
For some place cool where he could rest,
When over a well he saw what seemed best—
A bucket that old Mr. Man had made,
Hanging there in the afternoon shade.

But Riley had no sooner hopped into it
Than he in terror began to rue it,
For down toward the water went the bucket
And in a moment, kerplop! it struck it.

All this Brer Fox had seen with surprise,
Which is why he had blinked his greedy eyes.
Thought he, "I'll bet you that's where old Brer Bunny
Has got a keeping-place for his money,
Or else, just as sure as my nose is cold,
He's gone and discovered a whole lot of gold!"
With that he went over and looked in the well,
Then cupped his paws and gave out a yell:
"Hello, Brer Rabbit! What are you doing?
I've got a good mind to keep you there stewing!"

Now Riley was scared down there at the bottom,
But as for his wits, well he hadn't forgot 'em.
He sat very still in that old bucket,
Since he had no wish to tip it and duck it.
But he hollered back, "Hello, Brer Fox,
I'm doing real fine down here on these rocks,
For as sure as you're you and hens are all cluckers
I'm sitting down here a-fishing for suckers."

"Well tell me, Brer Rabbit, how're they biting?"
"Real fast, Brer Fox. They're keeping me fighting.
They're long and big and fun to catch.
Come on down and get you a batch."
"I know," said Brer Fox, "it's not very far,
But how do I get down there where you are?"
"Just jump in that bucket up there, and whee!
Down you will come. Go on and you'll see!"

Well almost Brer Fox's favorite dish
Was fried or broiled or just plain fish.
So in he jumped and down he went,
But this, of course, very quickly sent
Brer Rabbit's bucket up to the top,
Where he heard Brer Fox's bucket go plop!

And as they passed right plumb in the middle,
Brer Rabbit sang out like he heard a fiddle—
    "Good-by, Brer Fox,
    Take care of your clothes,
    For this is the way
    The whole world goes.
    Some go up
    And some go down.
    Be thankful you don't
    Just go roun' and roun'!"

Then with a frisky flip of his tail,
Brer Rabbit jumped out of Mr. Man's pail
And started to leave, but just to be nice
He left Brer Fox this word of advice:

"Mr. Man will be here, Brer Fox, pretty soon.
You'll hear him coming and whistling a tune.
But he always brings a great big gun,
So soon as he hauls you up—jump and run!"
With that Brer Rabbit took off with a swish
And left Brer Fox to catch all the fish.

BRER RABBIT'S VISIT TO AUNT MAMMY-BAMMY

   As lucky and smart as Brer Rabbit was,
He still had times, as everyone does,
When he felt low and stayed in his bed,
Afraid that some creature might stretch him out dead,
Brer Wolf or Brer Fox, or maybe Brer Bear,
And at such times he didn't much care.

Once, however, when he had the mopes,
Which was Riley's name for no-more-hopes,
He told Mrs. Rabbit that he had to journey
A long way away to see his attorney.
Now Mrs. Rabbit knew very well
What Riley meant, so on his lapel
She pinned a petunia and gave him a sack
Of cornbread and bacon to eat there and back.

Then Riley set out upon his journey,
Not indeed to see his attorney,
But off he went to the old Witch-Bunny,
The famous Aunt Mammy-Bammy Big-Money,
Who lived in a swamp where few rabbits had come,
And if you got there, you had to go some—
To ride some, slide some, jump some, hump some,
Hop some, flop some, walk some, talk some,
Creep some, sleep some, fly some, cry some,
Follow some, holler some, wade some, spade some—
And if you weren't lucky right up to your chin,
You weren't very likely to get there then.

When Riley arrived, having done his best,
He was all worn out, so he sat down to rest,
But pretty soon he called out loud and clear:
"Aunt Mammy-Bammy Big-Money—I'm here!
I've journeyed far and I've journeyed fast,
And once again I have found you at last."

At this a great big cloud of black smoke
Came up from the ground, and the Witch-Rabbit spoke:
"Son Riley Rabbit, Riley, son Riley,
Why have you come? You honor me highly."
"Aunt Mammy-Bammy, I've lost all my hopes
And go around all of the time with the mopes.
My thinking," said Riley, "is no longer quick
And I am no longer much good at a trick.
In fact, the truth is I'm just plain sick—
I'm woeful and weary and terribly worn
And in a blue funk, tormented and torn,
And if you can't find some potion to patch me,
Brer Fox or Brer Wolf will surely soon catch me."

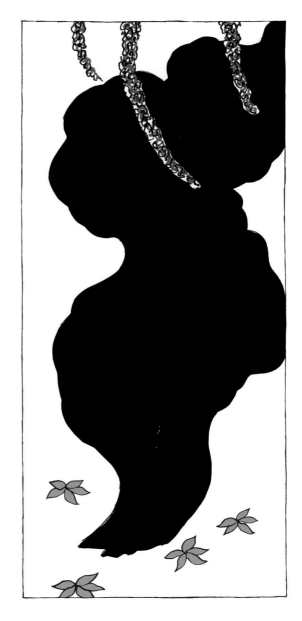

Then Aunt Mammy-Bammy came up from the ground
With more black smoke pouring out all around
And said, "Son Riley, there in that tree
Sits Bushtail the Squirrel—go fetch her for me."
At that Brer Rabbit studied awhile
And then, with just a wee hint of a smile,
He thought to himself, "I can do that much,
Even though I may have lost the old touch."

So lifting the sack of food he had taken,
He emptied out the cornbread and bacon,
And taking two rocks, he put the sack
Down over his head and most of his back
And sat down beneath the tree where Miss Squirrel
Was chatting away just like any girl.

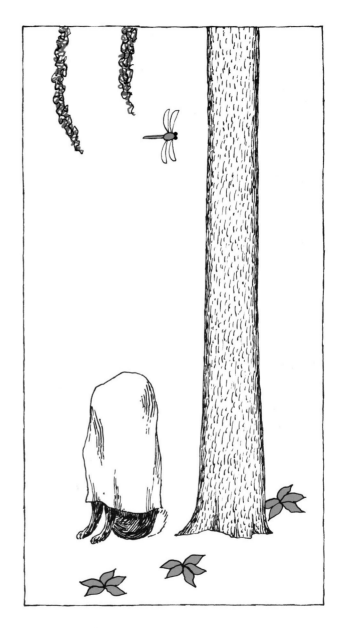

Then blip! he hit the two rocks together,
And Miss Bunny Bushtail wondered whether
She hadn't heard something down under her tree.
But she had decided she wouldn't go see
When all of a sudden something went blap!
As Riley gave his rocks a good slap.

And now Miss Bushtail ran down the tree
To see what that sound could possibly be,
And seeing the sack, she came to a stop
As Riley's two rocks hit each other—blop!

Then arching her tail in one big curl,
"Who's that?" said Miss Bunny Bushtail Squirrel.
"Just me," said Riley, "down here on the ground
Cracking some hickory nuts I found."
"Can I crack some?" Miss Bushtail inquired,
Which was, of course, what Riley desired,
And soon enough, in search of a snack,
Miss Bushtail was safe in Brer Rabbit's sack.

So fast that it was almost funny
He brought her to Aunt Mammy-Bammy Big-Money,
Who said, "Son Riley, off there I see
Brer Rattlesnake—go fetch him for me."
At this poor Riley's stomach felt queasy.
That test, he knew, would not be easy.
So once again he studied a bit
Until he felt he was ready for it.

Then going off in the bushes he got
A supple grapevine and made a slipknot,
With which he went up to Brer Rattlesnake
And asked how he was and was he awake.
Brer Snake looked sleepy and sore as a boil

And he drew himself up in a tighter coil
And flicked out his tongue as if it were greased
And showed very plainly that he was displeased.
"It slicks in and out," thought Riley, "but
That mouth of his still seems to be shut."

He didn't answer, at any rate,
So once again Riley threw out the bait,
With "Well, Brer Snake, I'm sure mighty glad
To meet up with you here, since I have just had
A big dispute with old Judge Bear.
We both agreed that no one can compare
With you for good looks—simply no one
When you are stretched out full length in the sun.
But he said you aren't but three feet long,
And I stood him down and said he was wrong.
I said that you were certainly four
Or four and a half feet long, and more!
I tell you, Brer Snake, he almost got a lick
Right smack on the back from my walking stick!"

Brer Rattlesnake still didn't make a reply,
But he uncoiled himself to lie
Stretched out in the sun, full length and slack,
Displaying the diamonds on his back.

"I told old Judge Bear," Brer Rabbit went on,
"That just as soon as he was gone
I'd make it a point of considerable pleasure
To find you somewhere and take your measure,
That is, Brer Snake, with your permission,
And if it won't be an imposition."
"Go on," said the Snake, "you're the mathematician.
Hurry up now and do your addition."

Swollen with pride, he stretched out as he spoke,
And he stretched so hard he almost broke,
While Riley stepped up, as if at his leisure,
To use his new grapevine rattlesnake measure.
And from the tail end he measured him there,
With "One foot, two foot, three foot for Judge Bear."

Then quickly he slipped the noose round the neck
Of Brer Rattlesnake and dragged the poor wreck
Through spots that were shady and spots that were sunny
To old Aunt Mammy-Bammy Big-Money.

But when he got there, she was not to be found,
Though she sent her voice up from the ground:
"If you had any more sense, Son Riley,
If you were even one bit more wily,
I tell you you'd be the ruination
Of everything in the whole creation!"

At this Brer Rabbit got back his high hopes
And almost at once he got rid of the mopes,
And now that he felt no longer low
He quickly let old Brer Rattlesnake go
And set out for home, singing a song,
And far though it was, he was there before long.